DUDLEY SCHOOLS LIBRARY
AND INFORMATION SERVICE

Five Teddy Bears

First published in 2007 by
Franklin Watts
338 Euston Road
London
NW1 3BH

Franklin Watts Australia
Level 17/207 Kent Street
Sydney
NSW 2000

A CIP catalogue record for this book is available from the British Library.

ISBN 978 0 7496 7149 5 (hbk)
ISBN 978 0 7496 7292 8 (pbk)

Series Editor: Jackie Hamley
Series Advisor: Dr Hilary Minns
Series Designer: Peter Scoulding

Printed in China

Franklin Watts is a division of Hachette Children's Books.

Five Teddy Bears

by Anne Adeney

Illustrated by Cathy Shimmen

Anne Adeney

"I sang 'Teddy Bears' Picnic' to my four little girls and their 300 teddies many times, so it's good to write their story!"

Cathy Shimmen

"I live in Cornwall with my husband, Paul. I've heard teddy bears like to picnic here but I haven't seen one yet! I had to imagine them for this book..."

Five teddy bears
go out of the door.

One meets a little girl.

Now there are four.

Four teddy bears
play in the tree.

One falls into a nest.
Now there are three.

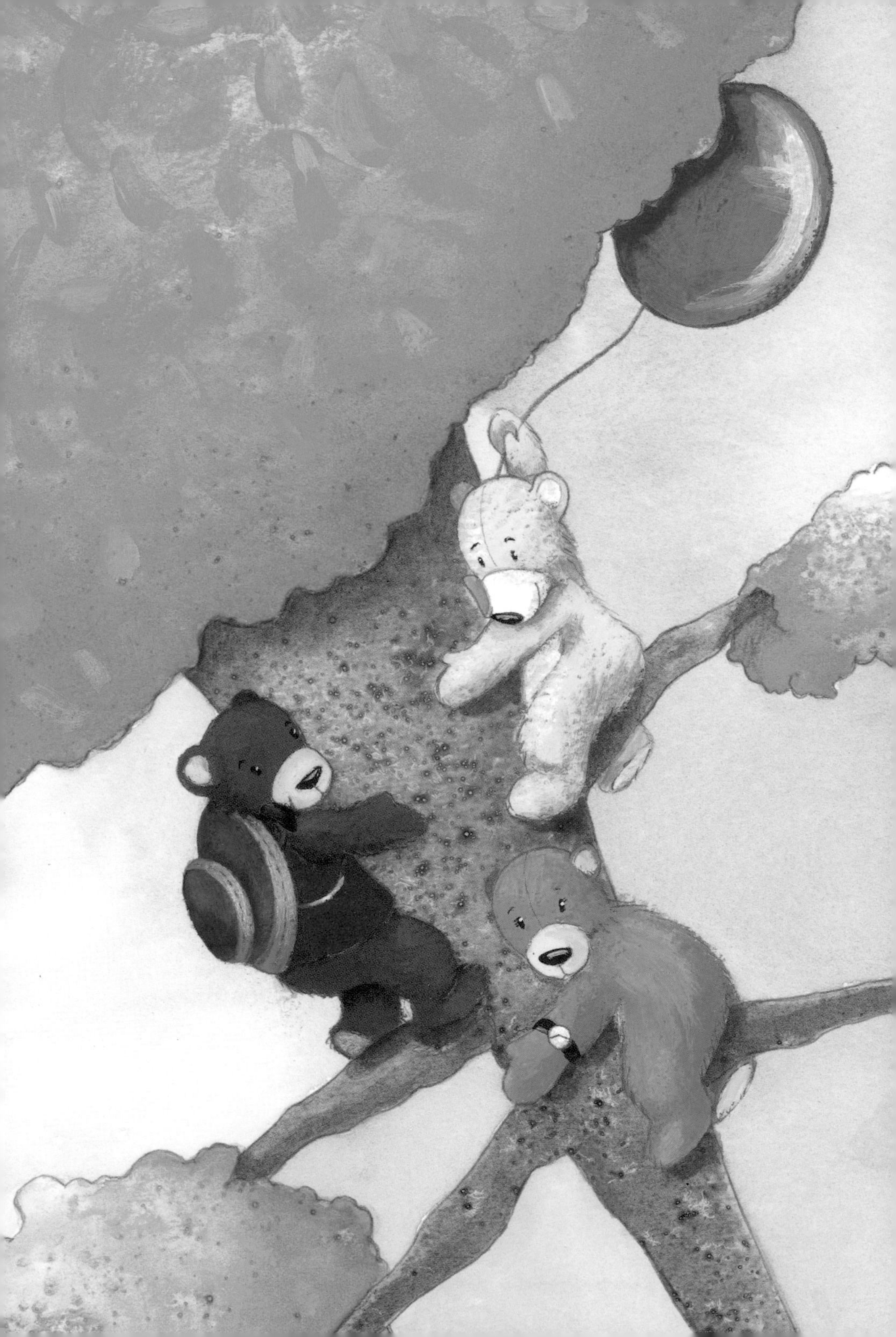

Three teddy bears
paddle a canoe.

One goes for a swim.

Now there are two.

Two teddy bears
begin to run.

One goes for a slide.

Now there is one.

So this teddy bear ...

... brings cake for everyone!

Notes for adults

TADPOLES are structured to provide support for newly independent readers. The stories may also be used by adults for sharing with young children.

Starting to read alone can be daunting. **TADPOLES** help by providing visual support and repeating words and phrases. These books will both develop confidence and encourage reading and rereading for pleasure.

If you are reading this book with a child, here are a few suggestions:

1. Make reading fun! Choose a time to read when you and the child are relaxed and have time to share the story.
2. Talk about the story before you start reading. Look at the cover and the blurb. What might the story be about? Why might the child like it?
3. Encourage the child to reread the story, and to retell the story in their own words, using the illustrations to remind them what has happened.
4. Discuss the story and see if the child can relate it to their own experience, or perhaps compare it to another story they know.
5. Give praise! Remember that small mistakes need not always be corrected.

If you enjoyed this book,
why not try another TADPOLES story?

Sammy's Secret
978 0 7496 6890 7

Stroppy Poppy
978 0 7496 6893 8

I'm Taller Than You!
978 0 7496 6894 5

Leo's New Pet
978 0 7496 6891 4

Mop Top
978 0 7946 6895 2

Charlie and the Castle
978 0 7496 6896 9

Over the Moon!
978 0 7496 6897 6

My Sister is a Witch!
978 0 7496 6898 3